This Orchard book

belongs to:

....

....

....

....

For Lewis – A.C.H.

For Michael, with love – A.P.

ORCHARD BOOKS
Carmelite House
50 Victoria Embankment
London EC4Y 0DZ

First published in 2014 by Orchard Books
First published in paperback in 2015

ISBN 978 1 40832 515 5

Text © Algy Craig Hall 2014 · Illustrations © Ali Pye 2014

The rights of Algy Craig Hall to be identified as the author and of Ali Pye to
be identified as the illustrator of this work have been asserted by them in
accordance with the Copyright, Designs and Patents Act, 1988.

A CIP catalogue record for this book is available from the British Library.

3 5 7 9 10 8 6 4 2

Printed in China

MIX
Paper from
responsible sources
FSC® C104740

Orchard Books
An imprint of Hachette Children's Group
Part of The Watts Publishing Group Limited
An Hachette UK Company
www.hachette.co.uk

THE DEEP DARK WOOD

Algy Craig Hall & Ali Pye

ORCHARD

This is the
deep dark wood.

There are lots of fierce and beastly creatures in the **deep dark wood** . . .

witches . . .

trolls . . .

giants...

and...

Look! Here comes a **sweet little girl**.
What is she doing in the **deep dark wood**?

Doesn't she know it's **DANGEROUS** here?

Oh, no!
The **big** bad wolf
has seen her.
This doesn't
look good.

"Hello," says the **big bad** wolf.
"Where are you going, you tasty . . .
I mean, **sweet little girl**?"

"I'm going to my best
friend's house for tea,"
says the little girl.

"You and your best friend are going to be MY tea," thinks the **big bad wolf**, licking his chops.

"Why don't I come with you to keep you safe?" says the naughty wolf. "A **deep dark wood** is no place for a sweet little girl, all on her own."

"Oh, thank you, Mr Wolf," says the little girl.

And together they set off, deeper into the **deep dark wood**.

"YIKES!" cries the little girl.
"Here's a witch coming to do horrible spells on us."

But the **big bad wolf** isn't even a little bit scared.

He *bristles*

and *grizzles*

and he scares that witch away.

"Oh, thank you, Mr Wolf," says the little girl, and they walk on, deeper into the **deep dark wood.**

Before long, the little girl cries out again. "HELP! There's a smelly old troll and he's coming to get us!"

The **big bad wolf** is a
tiny bit scared this time.

But he **bristles**

and **grizzles**

and **claws**

and
gnaws
and he
scares that
troll away.

"You're very brave, Mr Wolf," says the **sweet little girl,**
and they walk on, deeper into the **deep dark wood.**

"Uh-oh. Now we're really in trouble," whispers the sweet little girl. "Here's a hungry giant coming to gobble us up."

The **big bad wolf** really is scared this time.

But he bristles and grizzles and claws and gnaws and growls and howls

and WOW!
The **big** bad wolf manages
to scare that hungry giant away.

"Thank you very much for looking after me, Mr Wolf," says the **sweet little girl**. "Look, you've got us all the way to my best friend's house, safe and sound."

"I can't wait to eat . . . I mean **meet** her," chuckles the **big bad wolf**.

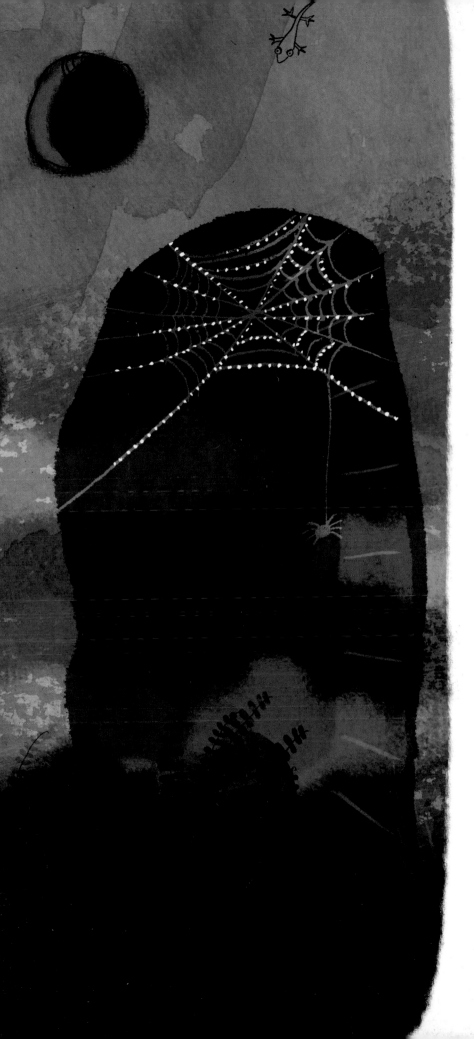

"But this is a funny place
for a little girl to live,"
says the wolf.

"Who said my best friend
was a little girl?"
says the sweet little girl.
"My best friend is . . .

...a big, scary

monster."

"Would you like a slice of cake?" says the sweet little girl.

But the wolf can't hear her.

He's running away as fast as he can, back into the **deep dark wood**.

Well, she is a VERY scary monster . . .

...but she's a **lovely** best friend.